Reading together is fun with
SHARE-A-STORY

A series specially designed to help you encourage your child to read. The right and left-hand pages are arranged so that you take turns and the story develops as a conversation. Fresh, humorous stories illustrated by top artists ensure enjoyment for everyone!

'Revolutionary ... done with as much good psychology as good humour ... Pat Thomson has contrived a set of readers likely to brighten bedtime for all parties' — *Mail on Sunday*

DIAL D FOR DISASTER

by

Pat Thomson

Illustrated by

Paul Demeyer

GOLLANCZ CHILDREN'S PAPERBACKS

There you are, Mum.
It's all right.
I've got everything ready
for Gran's birthday party.

What a day to be late.
I thought I'd better phone.
Could you hear me?
It was a terrible line.

Good. That's great.
I knew I could rely on you.
Did you make the beds?

Make the beds?
You said break the eggs.
I thought it was for omelettes.
They're all broken.

Oh dear.
Well, not to worry.
Did you shake the mat?

The mat?
You said shake the cat.
He was a bit annoyed.

Really!
What a thing to do!
What about the dusting?
Did you dust the ornaments?

Dust the ornaments?
I thought you said
bust the ornaments.
I know you don't like those vases.

Oh no! Worse and worse!
What about your socks then?
Did you wash your socks?

That explains it.
I was puzzled about that.
I washed the clocks.

Surely you got something right.
You put the soup in the saucepan?
You did that, didn't you?

Oh, soup!
It sounded like
put the soap in the saucepan.
It made lovely bubbles.

Heat the pies?
I heard eat the pies.
We've eaten them all up.

So there's no food.
And where's Sam?
Did you tell him
to tidy his cupboard?

Tidy his cupboard?
I thought you said
hide in his cupboard.
He's still in there.

This is ridiculous!
Get him out at once.
I suppose you forgot
Gran's birthday present.
Did you get the slippers?

Of course I didn't forget,
but you said flippers.
We bought her yellow flippers
for when she goes swimming.

Oh dear!
Where's the change?
Did you put the money
safely in my purse?

Money?
Not honey?
I poured the honey
in your purse.

It's a disaster!
Everything has gone wrong.
What shall we do?

Don't panic, Mum.
Just joking.
Everything is all right, really.
Come and see.

I almost believed you.
I shan't be late again.
My nerves won't stand it.

I did everything you said,
but why did we have
to wash our feet?
We both did it.

Feet? What feet?
It was a bad line, wasn't it?
I said did you want a treat.
Come on, call Sam.
We'll open it together
and then there will be
no mistakes!

First published in Great Britain 1990
by Victor Gollancz Ltd
First published in Gollancz Children's Paperbacks 1991

This new Gollancz Children's Paperbacks edition 1994
by Victor Gollancz
A Cassell imprint
Villiers House, 41/47 Strand, London WC2N 5JE

Text © Pat Thomson 1990
Illustrations © Paul Demeyer 1990

The right of Pat Thomson and Paul Demeyer
to be identified as authors of this work has been
asserted by them in accordance with the Copyright,
Designs and Patents Act, 1988.

A catalogue record for this book is
available from the British Library

ISBN 0 575 05759 9

Printed in Hong Kong